To Mimi and Jonathan, with love - TK

To bold Sir Alex and fair Lady May, with love - KR

Bloomsbury Publishing, London, Oxford, New York, New Delhi and Sydney

First published in Great Britain in 2016 by Bloomsbury Publishing Plc
50 Bedford Square, London, WC1B 3DP

A CIP catalogue record for this book is available from the British Library

ISBN 978 1 4088 4698 8 (HB)
ISBN 978 1 4088 4699 5 (PB)
ISBN 978 1 4088 4697 1 (eBook)

Printed in China by Leo Paper Products, Heshan, Guangdong

1 3 5 7 9 10 8 6 4 2

All papers used by Bloomsbury Publishing are natural, recyclable products
made from wood grown in well-managed forests.
The manufacturing processes conform to the environmental regulations of the country of origin

www.bloomsbury.com

BLOOMSBURY is a registered trademark of Bloomsbury Publishing Plc

SIR
DANCEALOT

Timothy Knapman
&
Keith Robinson

BLOOMSBURY
LONDON OXFORD NEW YORK NEW DELHI SYDNEY

In days of old, great tales were told
of fabulous fearless knights.
They fought all kinds of monsters
in tense and thrilling fights.

There was . . .

GEORGE
THE BOLD

KEN
THE MAD

and GEOFF
(who had an itchy bot).

But the bravest of them all was nimble-toed . . .

Sir Dancealot

When he saw a fearsome fiend,
he didn't shake or freeze.
NO!
He stood up straight,
and called out clear . . .

"Music, maestro, please!"

Then, before the beast attacked,
he'd grab it by the claw
and say, "Let's dance, my lovely!"
as he spun it round the floor.

He'd conga,

waltz

and

rumba

till the beastie's toes caught fire.

And it cried, "ENOUGH! No more!
You twinkle-toed live wire!"

He *boogied* off the bogglesnot,

he *jived* away a troll.

He beat three spotty ogres with
his non-stop rock 'n' roll.

And so the land was safe and free
and you could give the frights
to any passing monster
just by saying:

"DISCO LIGHTS!"

Until, that is, one winter's day
there came a fiery roar.
"Sir Dancealot!" the people cried.
"A dragon's at the door!"

It smelt far worse than pongy socks,
it reared up tall and fat,
with spikes and fangs and hairy bits,
and warts on where it sat.

"Sir Dancealot," it sneered, "you worm,
it's not your lucky day!
I know how you win all your fights
and so – I've learned ballet!

I can samba!

I can foxtrot!

I can hot cha-cha!

And of us two, I am the better
dancer here by far.

But just a simple dance-off?
I would beat you in a trice!
Therefore, to keep things interesting,
I say:

Let's dance

on

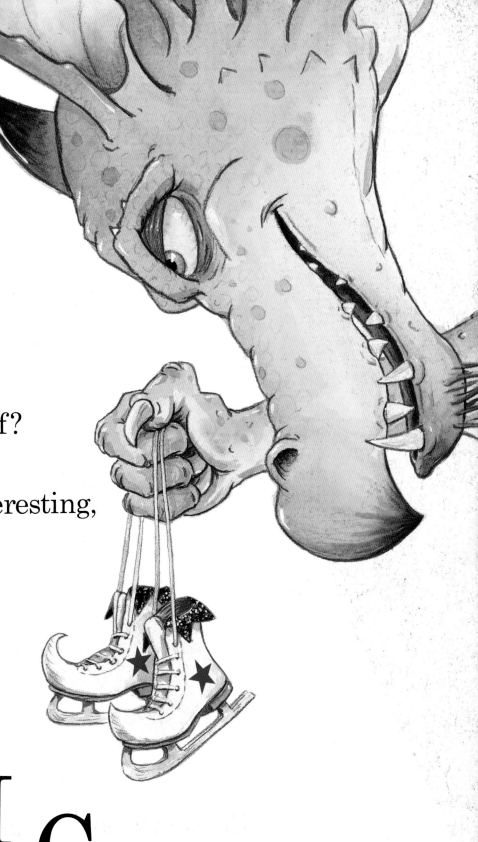

I C E!"

The castle moat was frozen
and Sir Dancealot felt glum.
He worried that he'd slip and slide
and fall flat on his bum.

"I must be brave!" he told himself,
"and face this dreadful foe!"
He looked it in its big green eyes
and said, "All right – let's go!"

The dragon grabbed Sir Dancealot so tight he thought he'd burst.
It did the tango on his toes and then – this is the worst . . .

it bopped

and locked

and body-popped

until its face went red.

Then grabbed Sir Dancealot
and whirled him
round and round
its head.

Sir Dancealot felt dizzy –
he knew he couldn't win!
He felt his feet begin to slip
and put him in a spin.

"My skates! I've lost my balance!"
Sir Dancealot cried out,
as he went sliding back and forth
and down and round about!

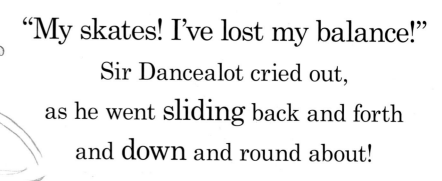

He **dragged** the dragon with him –
he wouldn't let it **go**!
"What are you **doing**, silly boy?"
the dragon **cried**,

"Oh, no!"

For as they both went sliding, their skates swished –

SLASH and SLICE

– and pretty soon they'd carved a great big hole in all that ice!

Then when Sir Dancealot let go –
the dragon couldn't stop!
It shot into the freezing water
with a dreadful plop!

"Sir Dancealot's our hero!"
the people cried, "Hooray!
He's beaten that
big scary beast
AND he's **saved** the day!"

The dragon **glugged**,
"**All right** you lot,
enough of **cheering** him!
I was so busy learning **dance**,
I **didn't** learn to **swim**!"

Sir Dancealot took pity, and he fished the dragon out.
He gave it something warm to wear and, as he dried its snout,
he had a great idea! He said, "Dear Dragon, you must stay!
And we'll be friends, and have such fun here each and every day.

I've never met a dancer who was half as good as you.
Just think of all the great and daring dances we could do!"

And from that day, the land was safe
from monsters and their threats.
Thanks to two unlikely friends –
and perfect pirouettes!